51 Poems

by
Edgar Ballantyne

Published by EBP
https://edgarballantyne.substack.com/

National Library of Australia Cataloguing-in-publication entry

Ballantyne, Edgar
51 Poems

ISBN 978-0-6486436-0-9 (paperback)
Cover design by Edgar Ballantyne, from his original photo
Printed and distributed by Ingram Spark
Typeset in Garamond

For

A, H and E
and JS
and MD

with the inspiration of Pádraig O Tuáma
and the crew of marvels that produce
Poetry Unbound

SECRETS 1

DREAMS 15

BLISS 27

PRAYERS 41

SONGS 55

SYMBOLS 65

SECRETS

Fire spiteful

Past the slanting cow dotted slopes
Ridge sneaking behind Ridge behind
Ridge, angling to the sky,
and past the softening into bush and
stutter-stepping into forest of the Earl
Grey trees
Smouldering and whispering over the hill
comes the Fire
Closer up it roars and tangles and writhes
Distantly it is brooding grudging sinister
Waiting for its time
Lies the fire

a theft

When the newsagent wasn't looking
I slipped it in my pocket
A camouflage coloured pen
Now, what sort of camouflage was it?
A much younger I
Many many planks of the ship now
carbuncled
And changed for others newer
You could've said, I wish I hadn't
You could've said it was wrong
But now I know it
I heard it from myself,
Earthquake, rumbled, my fingers and my
heart
And I located the fault line
An older boy dared me
I don't know if he saw me
or not

The food court

The food court
Where you are judge and jury of
The infra- burbling of a thousand
conversations
Curls and riptides of sound
Louder at high tide as they
tread water in the nagging pull of the
moon-mall
A cut-up tape of hastily glued fragments
of speech,
retrieved from the floor
Sprayed at distracting volume

The food court
Where one is greedy, and
Another got roast beef

The food court
To sift the claims of Battery and Salt
When prices attack
I apprehended violence, your honour
She got my spot in the line!
He stole the last cast iron pan
40% off, your honour!
The plaintive seeks injunction

The food court
Where 12 good men and true decide
If this skirt is really too short
If you can wear that to school, anyway
If it would attract wrong boys
If someone should invent an anti-wrong
boy spray, or simply mark their hands
with ink in a glove shape
If it could ever be what she was wearing
Objection!, Your honour, it's not a crime
to wear skirts
'I'll allow it' wrote the stenographer

The food court
Where 12 good men and true decide
Does my bum look big in this
Yes but darling, we want it to
Yes, darling, the bigger the better
Yes, always, darling

Little Taste

Just asleep
Like Lazarus under the rock
Just a slip
Like the Red Sea stepping aside
Just a little joke
Like the spear in the side
Just a touch on the arm
Like the nails on the cross
Just a little taste
Like communion wine, the blood for the
body
Just enough, she said
She said she's sure
And after all
Unjust

lovest

Limbic like a loose leash
A Limbo in a lovers leap
Talking with our bodies
Fingertips and signs of language
Breaths and inspirations
Following rumours of Atlantis
Somewhere under the waves
Following whispers of Shangri La
Emanating from the overlaid layers of
drawing and redrawing
On a lost and reused map
The whispers all at once can't distinguish
Or extinguish
The small needs can be said out loud
The great desires don't join to words
Perhaps, my darling, I can show you
Take you with me
Show and tell, go so slow and tell
Softly mixing our metaphors
in colder layers of the rising ocean

Anyone, but her

I can't believe what I'd done, officer
I never set out to do ____________
I can't believe-
It's so-
Please, don't call my mother
Anyone but her
Every woman could be a mother
Someone's mother
(Inaudible through sobs)
When I saw her with that note
I just felt so ________________
And that's how I went for the
____
And then she _________ from the house

That _________ _________
I told her so many times
Never to go to the ____________
We could _________ it out
And now, look what's happened
Me- a hard-working ___________
A _________ honest ____________
I can't believe it could have been
____
I'm not a ___________ person
Honestly

+ Roughly one Australian woman per
week is murdered in a domestic violence
situation
+ it keeps happening because we expect
   it, and let it

not being good enough

Goes to water, they said
It came to me
The brain is 70% water, mine was 100%
Seeping out onto my shirt, down my spine
Wasting opportunity, they said
No, it came to me
Chunks of land fell into the sea
And off they went to water
The erosion pattern of doubting,
doubting
Before too long, marooned
But the devil's bind stalks closer
Struggle and tighten the ropes
Let go and hold to nothing, to the sky

His world

When first of all he could hardly blink
An aperture for the entire world at once
Open
His world
My world
Everyone and anyone
Inflating like the Montgulfier balloon
A first flight rising to all worlds at once
But no eye at the centre
Except your I
Leading at least as far as you
                    (I have planted over winter)
were led

                              (over winter)
And bravely lurching further
                              (Below, below)
On the prow of a boat with
                    (Below the mother soil)
A hundred
                                   (for a time)
and one tiny soaking
                (that which will strain upwards)
pores below the waterline
            (Hopeful in the spring warmth)
Wicking and seeping
                          (Hoped-for warmth)

It's impossible to perfect
Impossible to do it wrong
Or any other way
It's possible to be imperfect
And sailing on
Sail on for sailing, for joy

DREAMS

**the analysis of dreams in which we are
slowly heading out to sea**

Between your land and my land
an ocean of dreams, gale-force
recollections
Placid bedtime murmurings

Was it better not to be enfolded, waved
away you let yourself go out to sea
See it now, bopping away over the waves,
kayak upturned,
Shark-teeth rocks, opening wide to ingest
You thought you were helping by clinging
tighter and tighter, till the crying stopped
You were, but you were helping yourself
As a windscreen wiper dismisses

Tell me how to be good, she pleaded
Guilty, Tell me what to do
Simply stop trying, and be, and wait
And be
And weight
Some implicit denial in that statement
It's take-your-grievance to work day
Sneak some grievances out the
photocopier for the children to draw on

I show you with my hands how the head
is above this line
And the emotion is below, in the body
And I show you with my hands
How the line can be up to your chin, the
point of your nose
And then you slip below the amniotic
surface
The internal amniotic ocean

You've only just got to the source
Don't rush to explain it away, away

In the Wind

In the wind between, the grass stalks
I heard a whispered Symphony

In the bruised and peach, fluorescent
clouds
I saw a playful child smudging

In the Fire tantalising, the Fields of Gold
I saw the light and let it be

how did I get here?

As I wander into sleep
I slip my thoughts into the deep
Blizzard slopes of sharp and steep
A phantom of this shadow leap

embarrassment

We[]<[]><[]><[]><[]><[]><[]><[]><[]
We laugh <[]><[]><[]><[]><[]><[]><[]
We laugh it <[]><[]><[]><[]><[]><[]>[]
We laugh it off <[]><[]><[]><[]><[]>[]
We laugh it off forever <[]><[]><[]><[]
We (always) <[]><[]><[]><[]><[]><[]>
We (always) laugh<[]><[]><[]><[]><[]>
We (always) laugh (but)[]><[]><[]><[]>
We (always) laugh (but) it[]><[]><[]><[]
We (always) laugh (but) it (sounds) []><[]
We (always) laugh (but) it (sounds) off<[]
We (always) laugh (but) it (sounds) off
(pitch)
We (always) laugh (but) it (sounds) off
(pitch) forever

Over the side

A Frankenscene
A low fire along the scrub grass stalks
Smoke listing windward, outrunning the
fire
I escape in a balloon with bicycle bellows
You open the sandwiches, but I keep
dropping them over the side
My hands won't cooperate
Crows tornado inside the balloon but peel
out and scrap for these offerings
We slip towards the smoke and the ocean
The fields and stalks smoke and leisure
their way down the cliff side
As cotton would fall from a table
Briefly I could not say which part was
moving
The fields and stalks spread themselves
over the water
Colours mixing over the waves
The sky split and unrolled into negatives
Burning celluloid
And behind this the red giant Antares
Into which we drifted forever

surely some mistake

As the earth slipped over the sun
The midnight midday black
Of a wayward accusation
Slipped over my soul
Entranced in shadow
I felt only one thing
I can be condemned
But not for this

In memory of Trace Vanadium

In a pinch and a bubble, someday
There will be no more living
I'll stop, but you should go on
I saw a great Vaporator machine
Like a sky burial it vaporises and separates
The Useful
I am next on the conveyor belt, that's all
In the human body, I learn
There are 65 scents of oxygen
You can borrow if you like
18.5 scents of carbon
For which I'd like to be the brakes in a
very fast race car
10 scents of hydrogen
Use these for green steel, or wafting
refugees atop the Mediterranean in a
renewable fashion
3.2 scents of nitrogen
Set aside just for laughs
1.6 scents of calcium, oh calcium, you
alkaline tart
Set my bones for now and Mayan temples
for eternity
1 scents of Phosphorus
Keep these to rhyme with Bosporus

0.4 scents Potassium, in a pre-recorded
voice
'Please make available for spacecraft
breathing apparatus'
0.25 scents of sulfur, for powdering guns
and making Hogmanay fires work in the
sky
0.2 scents of sodium, to clean ink, to
make paper blank anew
0.2 scents of chlorine, which I hope
You'll use to keep things clean
0.04 scents Magnesium
To support the grip of free solo climbers
up Denali, and other ascendings
0.006 scents of Iron must be magnetised
to guide the Monarch Butterflies
0.004 scents of zinc with which
I'd like to silently shield a hull someplace
further North
0.001 scents of silicon, which should a
future supermodel grace
Somewhere not round enough for her,
but good enough when I am done
And for the traces, just change my name
to something real exciting like
Trace Vanadium

more waking

We dream more waking than asleep
In the stretching of the bow
In the throwing of stones
to ripple the surface of the world
Beginning over and over we must
From loose threads and from dust
The steam and smudge of what came just
before these opaque guesses
While all the shadow seamstresses
Begin again into the dusk
And cities shimmer out of floating ashes

BLISS

Quiet, souls

A curly dark lad in a high red leather chair
Breathing to slow the everything
Sprung forward in all their seats
The audience take with him the inevitable
leap
Their energy of expectation
An electromagnetic field of bliss
He cannot help but close the circuit
Through only him with as least resistance
As may be, as may be
5,000 quiet souls attending to their
harmony
To the tender oscillations of the bow
The humming vibrato loosening the latch
on the cello
Be so gentle as a lover, slip it free
Now, the butterfly enclosure is open to
the public
They flutter out by the F-hole
Behold the bliss of music
The butterflies of almost lucency

Dance

Stay still
For the earth to dance underneath you
Still, my friend, the Earth

Softly balance
For the strain to flow all around you
Stress in the syllables, softly
The stress, my friend, we need

Step lithe
For the hope to show your course
As the river runs fearful, of course
No mistakes here
Mis-takes, my friend, are the course

theatre

It started as nothing at all
Four parallel fabric waves
Careful hands pulsing
Dashing back and forth the stage
It took on the breath of life
Instigation
Inspiration
Invitation
The crowd held a breath
Suspending the action
Held the cast aloft
All souls united and incorporated
All the merely players, sustained

The next beginning was a tumble of long
army coats
Taken turn by turn to the shoulders
Hoisting false covers to the wind
Disguises doffed, selves on-and-offed
But
You can't put your guilt in the ground
And Oh, how sin beget sin
How the sin gets in
And the sun forgets some
Of the faces of fathers

And shapes the shadows they show
It's a form of hypnosis, really
Smoke, spells, horrors, and dreads
All suggested, All invoked
All the Scottish players entrained

Painting

On a straining frame of work, a day
squabbles
As tarmac white dashes guard, the cirrus
parapets
Whereby
Gloss silver panels mould a spaced row
of green evers
The sleepy arrogance of sunset creeps the
stipple rock hillside
As roadkill submit to the winter moon
Full, round, imperious
As white, wheeled transit of urgent blood
delivery and mauve gilding the horizon
Somewhere catecholamines dawdle and
potholes erupt the road
Stratified strain on stress on exhaustion
of detailed attention as streetlights foster
blinking circuitry
As crochets quaver the hours and minutes
only forwards, only forwards

raking Zen garden

On Mondays, the sand directs the rake
just like this
Into righteous runs and rows
Nothing to do with me
Me with nothing to do

for where else could it go?

On Tuesdays, the sand
Spirals up toward enlightenment
And when it gets there does what it was
doing before
Grains counting time

On Wednesdays,
The sand wants to join the wind as if they
were really ever separate
And they point to each other without
names
And abrade away expectations

On Thursdays, I can hardly lift the rake
Not because it is too heavy, but because it
is too light
Because there are glimpses of the view
where there is nothing separate

No sand, rake, temple, tasks
Just whatever is is

On Fridays, I am scolded by the Roshi
For not realising the obvious
That I am sand and rake and wind and so
is he
And all are safe beyond words
But no one has swept the sand back in
He throws it in my face with compassion

On the weekend, the sand can be looked
at but is far too pure to touch

the very last second before

We were about to be
Intwined and softly folded like pillowing
double helix ivy
and also
The bark of a new log catching onto the
smouldering heat rumour,
glowering and spitting the name of the
universal fire
and also, so also, o so slow
mainline Adrenaline from the bat-cave
brain-stem sauna
and also
A newborn green leaf unfurling proud
into the spring breeze, frogs quirk-
quirking as the morning awakes

on leaving the ground

At last, degravitation
But first, in order
Thinking through
Surfaces; intact
Combustion; twirling
Controls; obeying
Pressures; rising
Temperatures; rising
Complying with the laws of physics
And then, and then

Inertia
Revolutions
Rotations
Propulsion
Pitching

…………… lift
………………….. ascent
…………………………………..freedom

Oh, but temporary freedom

Entering the ocean

Cold that killed the dinosaurs still lurking,
the ocean

Power curls and crashes the source of all
sources, the ocean

Sun glistening just for you as you spread
your arms, the redeemer, the ocean

Floating like afterglow with your lover,
the ocean

Oh, such bliss, the ocean

In the flow

We took her straight to theatre
I saw the bruising
Stained flank, abdominal bleed
We stepped through   incisions
The suture ……………………….. The
artery
I   Was   The   artery
I   Am   The   Artery
The   Ah   -te   -ree
tha-   Tree
Art-   Ree
Arrr-   eee
r e

Round poem
(choose a path, and later on pretend it was
an accident)
(later on choose another path, and turn
over old stones)

In a wandering afternoon

          because you said we should, but I
               wouldn't

as we candled the coals of our blessings

lingering like the waves of a little bang

          over and over and around the edges

since ten-past forever

     while shaking the gold flecks from the
                    stones

we sat and whistled the old cheerful songs

PRAYERS

Faith

A wish twinned with a verb
the path through forest to morning
believing yourself
A parachute filling jolt
seeing y o u r s e l f
sunlight fingers on your cold shoulder
hearing y o u r s e l f
peaceful sigh of snowflakes
knowing y   o   u   r   s   e   l   f

for strength   43

Strong
-are the minded
-are the willed
-are the hearted
-are the open
like sand into glass

for charity

The ice shroud of morning, to water, and
to water

The cracked-in car, by the highway
Festive police tape for windows
Parts donating themselves to passers-by
Carburettors and so on, and so on

The cut stump, waiting spring of
sprouting
Mother's metacarpals clawing out of the
ground
The night-kissed child, cosseting the
morning

clemency

Everything other kept moving
I stood still
Rosella leaped red-bleen-grue off the
seed, dog-twitching
Fog whispered over the scattered play-
blocks of town
Night heaved-ho over the sea and hoist
the darkness landward
Worlds-worths of graveyards sat seminary
cemetery centenary silent
The Pacific Plate shrugged its enormous
old shoulders
Khumbu creaked and rumbled over last
season's avalanchees
Earth whirled a little further, pursuing all
of our Sun
I shouldn't have said it
The hornet hummed near my ear
I stood still, aye

justice

You do not see it in the mother Africa
With child, whose eyes do not shine
Lethargy in effigy
To know there is enough for anyone, and
sometimes everyone
You do not see it in the shuffling coal
dust of an unemployment line
You do not see it in the slow rehearsal of
polar ice

You see it in the last glistening drop of
eternity before the hourglass turns back
again
You see it in the thousand-fold rings of
bristlecone methuselah

You feel it
And where you feel it
Is how you know your soul is there and
where it is

lead me not into envy

The thing I most want is not to want
What a folder paper soul this would be
What a footwell receipt this would be
Crumpled, deranged, the weak old ink
scared away by the sun
And what did I even spend on it, illegibly?
And what use a library borrowing slip?
Dates in burgundy and turquoise
Whole years sometimes in-between
Stamp your soul for re-entry

Try, says the meme, wanting what you got
And this would be a wanting too, and all
A closed loop
Where begging is out of the question

clariticking

Does a clock really know what it's doing?
The marking of ticks and tocks
Does the second hand yearn?

But nobody wants to be a cog
Grinding as the saying goes exceedingly
fine, the joy out of life
Every thing is exceedingly fine
We want the mechanism
But are surprised at time running out
Running out
Marching out
Finding out
Time is exceedingly fine
Grinding out the instants, moments
Leaving these aside
Discarding them for not enough time

guidance

A straight yellow line along a ribbon black
road
A remote desert road
Where the cactus of morality is scarce
and spiny
Crows wheel freely overhead, simply
waiting, waiting
But oh, the sands are mischievous
The wind wanders them out of their place
The wind wanders down the dunes
The sand meanders into the air
Grain by grain
Speck by speck
Covers the tarmac
Such as was the road, erode
A man covered in sores and the sores in
bandages
Follows the line but loses the way
Braille foot out in front for the tar
Braille hand seeking what is meant by the
moving sand
Delirium visits
Now they are dunes of old paper
Millenia of ink, never more parched than
parchment

The wind and the sun disintegrate this
wisdom
Disinter, dissipate, and disparage
The parchment and the wind leave the
ground, gathering lift
No longer parchment but fragment
Heraclitus and the bard dance a rising jig
The sore man ceases and waits, thirsty

growth

In the slightly lucid veined canopy
twinkling the wind
In the sinew crucible of reaching soaring
oak arms
In the tenacious plaque of two
generations' lichen
In the crafty-waltzing, night summoning
shadows
In the slithering ebony fingers yearning
into the dark leaf rot soil
There spreads the magnificent aftermath
of 20,000 days

forgiveness

For	giving
For	going
For	getting
For	knowing
For	living
For	letting
For	loving
For	showing

For	shadowing
For	shining
For	shaming
For	locking

For	stalling
For	nearing
For	fearing

Of falling

And picking your jigsaw self
piece by piece

For	knowing
For	going
For	giving
For	getting

For   showing
For   letting
For   loving
For   living

For no one
Who can know it
But you

SONGS

hope

As a set theory
As a relaying medley of persons
Why do we like stories that we know
aren't true?
And what can an imagination do that
It hasn't already done

As a string theory of secret dimensions
And other kinds of persons
Why do we contradict ourselves saying
reality tv deeper and deeper into the
night?
As we hear the pulsing alarm of the
meteorite approaching
As days hour into minutes
We will know it was a story

survival

The ambulances come tooting in full
And leave barren empty
For out there are more, many more

The needle slips in so easily
You'd never even know
The field of poppy heaven sways so slow
You'd almost never know

The bone ache came early today
Racing dawn down the yard
The crab has its ragged grip
But to live, or to love
That urge was like that when I got here

intermittent slowing

Mobile conversation ruffles the oak leaves
of the park
One way, as usual
If plants can absorb vibrations and grow
better when praised,
If hot air mainly rises and leaves the earth
If the spaces between moments are so
much more space than moment
Then what is sequestered in these shady
chieftains?
And as the light suffuses their leaves
Is the truth strained out of them again?
And if the globe keeps turning
Will past chances see another summer?

Heart

At the centre of everything
(You ever knew was louder than bible
truth)
(In the latening light as we gorgeously
vowed)
(While the leaf herald of autumn was
briefly concentrated between sun and soil)
(And over the edge of collapsing
possible)
While your heart and mine gallop through
time
And in time

Dedication

We burn in the sight of the sun
This world dispersed by ultraviolet
Flake by flake into the past
Great sheet music of the world unfolds
One more turn each year
Would you rather play,
Or turn it backwards to keep it forever

Jealousy

You belong to me
Which cannot ever be true
As rain cannot rise

sky

The sky separated into droplets and
folded down into the horizon
It was pretty obvious, the world was
ending
Or at least beginning to end
Clouds cricked and cracked, resisting
Deciding whether to break or bend
It goes like that
From beginning to end,
and then
they all fell down in raptures

soaring

As the eagle flies
Lifting up by speed and pitch
Like our metal wings

heat   64

The fires lies under oath to the wood
This won't hurt a bit
The wood lies in the fire
And then escapes into the sky

SYMBOLS

edge

Step to a cliff edge
And you will see your limit
For the need to thrill

desire

Summer Winter Autumn Spring
Saunter Swimmer Enter Swing
Simmer of the sweetest fling
I give you all that I can bring

rage
                    68

In the museum of frozen retribute
Even the painting
of an ice shelf is dripping
Walls cannot contain the rise
But yet a museum there is

care and despair

It's not whether I tell you
If there are no words for it
But whether there is elastic
Without bands

nurturing

A scrubbed and weathered man sat at the
microphone
Volleying questions
An enormous network, you say, of rest
huts funded by donations and by our
foundation?
Yes, exactly that, sir
On the main route all around this
country?
Correct, sir
For what purpose?
It would allow devoted pilgrims to walk
all the way around the country without
needing food or clothing
But why?
I cannot tell them that
Only they can tell me why they do it
BUT WHAT WOULD IT COST?
It would cost less than the gain, sir
They will discover something about
themselves, about our country and about
time itself by seeing it on foot
And what would that be?
I do not know, it has not been discovered
yet
Sorry, but what would they do?

They would wash their clothes and
blankets, let them dry and take fresh ones
They would eat the simple food available
They could not possibly know why, until
after they have done it

play

In a narrow slip
Above hills, below night cloud
Orange spring moon winks

Edgar Ballantyne is old enough to
know better, and lives in Australia
with his wife and two terrific
children. He works at a hospital,
where he does whatever he can, as
much as he can, if he thinks it will
help. He likes poetry because it's the
shape that thoughts come in anyway.
He intends to complete various prose
projects, and sighs when he realises
he hasn't. He is also a keen runner
and photographer, and loves
throwing the ball and watching the
dog bring it straight back, while the
dog loves sitting and watching for
him to throw the ball again.

www.ingramcontent.com/pod-product-compliance
Lightning Source LLC
Chambersburg PA
CBHW061109100726
47911CB00012B/467